USBORNE HOTSHOTS

WORLD HISTORY DATES

USBORNE HOTSHOTS

WORLD HISTORY DATES

Lisa Miles and Anne Millard
Designed by Fiona Johnson

Series editor: Judy Tatchell
Series designer: Ruth Russell

Note on the dates

The year 0 is taken as the year of Christ's birth. BC after a date means "before Christ". AD (*anno domini* – Latin for "the year of the Lord") means after His birth. Dates for which no letters are given are AD.

When dates appear with a "c." before them, this means that the date is not certain. The "c." stands for *circa*, which is Latin for "about".

c.10,000BC
Farming begins

Wild wheat

Farmed wheat

Wild sheep

Farmed sheep

When the climate grew warmer around 12,000 years ago, people began to breed animals and grow plants for their food. Before this time, they had hunted animals and gathered plants. As farming grew, people also built permanent shelters instead of moving around.

Farming first began in an area of the Middle East known as the Fertile Crescent. The area had rivers for water and was ideal for farming.

c.8000BC
Jericho – the first town

One of the earliest towns in the world was called Jericho, in the Middle East. It flourished around 8000BC. Its people grew rich and built walls around their town to protect themselves. At one time, over 2,000 people lived in Jericho.

c.3500BC
The Sumerian civilization

Gradually civilizations developed. Civilizations are organized societies, with writing systems. The people do specific jobs and are ruled by leaders. The first civilization was that of Sumer in the Middle East, which began around 3500BC. By 3100BC, three cities had developed – Ur, Uruk and Eridu.

This Sumerian decorated panel is known as the Royal Standard of Ur.

The Sumerians made objects out of copper and pottery. They also made cloth. Traders journeyed as far as Turkey and and even India to exchange goods with other peoples. The Sumerians were a highly inventive people. As well as inventing writing, they devised a legal system and were skilled mathematicians and astronomers. They had hundreds of gods and goddesses.

A Sumerian temple, called a ziggurat, for religious worship

Egypt unites

In 3100BC, the two Egyptian kingdoms of the Lower and Upper Nile were united by the pharaoh Menes. "Pharaoh" is the word for an Egyptian king.

The kingdoms first arose around 3300BC, from farming communities that grew up along the Nile.

People migrate

Between 3000-2000BC, there were great movements of peoples around Europe and Asia. Many drifted into the Middle East, where some settled, while others moved on. Many belonged to one of two main language groups – Semitic and Indo-European, from which many modern languages are descended. Arabic and Hebrew are Semitic languages. Most modern European languages are Indo-European.

Egypt – the Old Kingdom

One of the greatest periods of Ancient Egyptian history was called the Old Kingdom, which lasted from c.2649BC until 2150BC. The pyramids (tombs of the pharaohs) were built during this time.

The Indus Valley

The first great Indian civilization spread along the Indus Valley, beginning around 2500BC. Its leading cities were called Harappa and Mohenjo-Daro. The cities were large and surrounded by defensive walls of baked brick. They had central areas called citadels, built on raised mounds.

Indus goddess

Egypt – the Middle Kingdom

After the Old Kingdom, Egypt was disunited and suffered a period of trouble. Then followed the Middle Kingdom, which lasted from c.2040BC to 1640BC. During this time, the princes of Thebes came to power and reunited Egypt. They conquered Nubia to the south and built a chain of huge brick fortresses to protect their new frontier.

The Great Pyramid at Giza

The Sphinx – an ancient Egyptian monument

Zoser's Step Pyramid at Sakkara

c.2000BC
The Minoans

The first great European civilization developed on the island of Crete around 2000BC. The people are known as the Minoans, after a legendary king called Minos. Traders, craftsmen and artists were based around a number of large palaces, such as the one at Knossos. The Minoans went abroad and traded. Some of them could read and write.

Minoan wall-painting

c.1900BC
The Mycenaeans

From c.1900BC, the people of Greece had their own civilization. We call it the Mycenaean civilization after Mycenae, the leading state. The Mycenaeans lived in small kingdoms, and shared the same culture and language. Each kingdom had its own city, which was usually built on high ground with walls to defend it.

Gold mask of a Mycenaean king

c.1490BC
Tuthmosis III reigns

The Egyptian Empire grew to its greatest extent during the reign of the pharaoh Tuthmosis III (c.1490-1436BC),

during the New Kingdom period. In all, he fought 17 campaigns of war against foreign powers.

Tuthmosis III

1347BC
Tutankhamun – the boy king

Egypt's most famous pharaoh is Tutankhamun. He became king when he was only about nine years old in 1347BC. He only reigned for ten years.

Tutankhamun's body was found inside these four coffins. The funeral mask (below left) is a portrait of the king.

His fame comes from the fact that in 1922, his tomb was discovered packed with incredible treasures that had lain undisturbed for over 3,000 years.

Ramesses II reigns

Ramesses II reigned from 1289-1224BC. He lived until he was over 90 and was a great warrior king. He claimed that the god Amun was his real father and built temples throughout Egypt and Nubia. The two temples cut into the rock at Abu Simbel were built by him.

Abu Simbel

The Sea Peoples attack

In Greece, bad harvests, famine and loss of trade led the Mycenaean way of life to collapse. A large fleet sailing around the Mediterranean in 1190BC may have included Mycenaean refugees. The Egyptians called them the Sea Peoples. The Sea Peoples attacked cities, but were eventually defeated by the Egyptians. After this they spread out around the Mediterranean.

Greece itself entered a period called the Dark Ages, when many skills, such as writing, architecture and making pottery, declined or were lost.

The Kingdom of Israel

Under Kings Saul and David, the Isrealites defeated the Philistines in c.1005BC and set up the Kingdom of Israel in Canaan, with Jerusalem as its capital. The Israelites were a group of Semitic tribes who had established themselves in Canaan in the Middle East in c.1200BC. They were united by their belief in one God. In later times, the kingdom split in two – Israel in the north and Judah in the south.

The Olmec civilization

The first civilizations to appear in America began around 1000BC. Among the first civilized people were the Olmecs, from Mexico. They constructed religious buildings and carved huge stone heads. They used a type of picture writing and also used calendars.

A giant Olmec head carved from rock

753BC
Rome begins

In Latium, the central plain on Italy's west coast, a group of villages grew up around a river called the Tiber. According to legend, it was in 753BC that Rome was founded by Romulus after he killed his twin brother Remus. Romulus was Rome's first king.

In legend, Romulus and Remus were suckled by a wolf.

605BC
Nebuchadnezzar rules

Babylon was one of the greatest cities of the ancient world. The Babylonian Empire was at its height during the reign of King Nebuchadnezzar, from 605 to 562BC. Nebuchadnezzar built a huge, terraced ziggurat and planted it with trees and bushes. It became known as the Hanging Gardens, and was one of the ancient Seven Wonders of the World. The empire was invaded by the Persians in 539BC and then became part of the Persian Empire.

The Ishtar Gate in Babylon

490BC
The Persian Wars begin

In 490BC, war broke out between the Greek city of Athens and the mighty Persian Empire. The Persians wanted to punish Athens for helping other Greek cities to try to break free from them. The Persian forces landed at Marathon, where the Athenians managed a surprise victory.

8

In 480BC, the Persians returned and destroyed Athens. The Athenians, though, finally defeated the Persians in 479BC.

A Persian archer from the sixth century BC

431BC
The Peloponnesian War

Greek communities were divided into small states called city-states. Each had their own laws, armies and money, but they shared the same language and culture. In 431BC, the Peloponnesian War broke out between Athens and Sparta – two powerful city-states. Sparta eventually won the war, but its arrogance and brutality turned the other Greek cities against it. Athens later recovered its former power to become the leading Greek city.

336BC
Alexander the Great

In 336BC, Alexander the Great came to power in Greece. He went on to conquer the largest empire that the world had ever known until that time.

Alexander's empire included Persia and Egypt and he marched through Africa and Asia, founding many cities, which were called Alexandria after him. He eventually died in Babylon in 323BC. His empire was divided up among his generals.

Alexander the Great from a Roman mosaic

c.280BC
The Pharos lighthouse

During the reigns of Alexander's successors, the Pharos lighthouse in Alexandria, Egypt was built around 280BC. It was one of the ancient Seven Wonders of the World.

For hundreds of years after Alexander's death, Greek culture and language dominated an enormous area. This era was known as the Hellenistic Age.

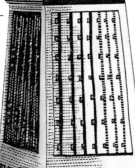

The Pharos lighthouse. It was over 100m (300ft) high.

264BC
The Punic Wars begin

Rome steadily became the dominant power in Italy. In 264BC, it came into conflict with the great city of Carthage in North Africa. Rome and Carthage fought a series of wars, called the Punic Wars. In the second Punic War, a Carthaginian general named Hannibal marched over the Alps from Spain with an army of elephants to attack Italy. In the third Punic War, the Romans destroyed Carthage.

259BC
The first Emperor of China

In 259BC a man called Zheng became king of the province of Qin in China. He united China under his rule and took the

Zheng (above) and the Great Wall (left)

name Shih Huang Ti, which means "First Emperor of China". He began work on the Great Wall of China to protect his territory from enemies. The wall is the largest man-made structure in the world.

49BC
Caesar comes to power

In 49BC, Julius Caesar seized power in Rome and became the most powerful ruler it had ever had. He made many reforms which were popular, but some people became worried because he made decisions without consulting the Senate (the government of Rome). On March 15, 44BC, Caesar was stabbed to death by a group of conspirators.

Caesar's heir took power and became the first Roman Emperor, Augustus. He set up a military dictatorship which lasted for 500 years.

The end of Ancient Egypt

Egypt was conquered by the Persians, who in their turn were conquered by Alexander the Great in 332BC. As a result, Egypt became part of his Greek Empire. After Alexander's death, it was ruled by a new family of rulers called the Ptolomies. It eventually fell to the Romans in 30BC after the suicide of Queen Cleopatra and her Roman husband Mark Antony.

Maya warrior

The Maya

The Maya, who lived in Mexico, entered their greatest period around AD250. They believed their kings were gods. The god-kings celebrated their own importance by building cities and monuments to themselves. They also used picture writing and were astronomers and mathematicians.

Rome at its peak

The Romans continued to build their empire, conquering land in Asia, Europe and Africa. The empire was at its height during the reign of Emperor Trajan in AD117. His victories in Dacia (modern Romania) are recorded in a series of sculptures on a pillar in Rome known as Trajan's Column.

Trajan's Column

Barbarians invade

In the fourth century, a tribe of warriors called the Huns invaded Europe from Asia. They drove before them the tribes of central Europe, who the Romans called barbarians. In AD367, they poured across the Rhine into the Roman Empire and began to set up kingdoms. The Roman Empire began to crumble.

Shield, spear and helmet of a barbarian

391
Christianity in Rome

In 391, Christianity became the official religion of the Roman Empire. In earlier periods, it had been discouraged and at times was banned. Christians were often persecuted or killed. In 312, Emperor Constantine (306-337) was said to have seen a vision of the Christian cross before he went into battle and from this time, he encouraged the religion.

A Christian inscription on a Roman tomb

527
The Byzantine Empire

The Roman Empire in western Europe collapsed. In the east, it survived and flourished as the Byzantine Empire, around the city of Constantinople (modern Istanbul). Gradually it gained its

The Emperor Justinian, from a Byzantine mosaic

own identity and became Greek in culture. In 527 Emperor Justinian regained some of the old Roman territories in the west, but his conquests were lost within a century.

570
Birth of Muhammad

The great religion of Islam was founded by Muhammad who lived from 570 to 632. He claimed that he received messages from Allah (God), and preached that his fellow Arabs should submit to Allah's will. Allah's words, known as the Ko'ran, became the principles of the religion of Islam.

In 622, Muhammad and his followers arrived in Medina in Arabia, after being forced out of Mecca. This date marks the birth of Islam. People who follow the religion of Islam are called Muslims.

618
The T'ang Dynasty begins

In 618, China came under control of a family of rulers called the T'ang Dynasty. The T'ang era became one of the greatest

A glazed T'ang Dynasty camel

periods of Chinese history. Printing, porcelain, paper money and gunpowder were all invented during this time. In 907 the T'ang Dynasty fell to invaders and China entered a troubled period.

700
West African empires

From around 700, fabulously rich empires existed in West Africa. They were rich because of their supply of gold. Arab traders bought salt from the Saharan salt mines, then carried it to towns where they sold it for gold and slaves. These amazing empires were: Ghana, which thrived until around 1200; Mali, which thrived from 1200 to 1500; and Songhai, which existed from around 1350 to 1600.

Timbuktu – a West African trading city

750
Islam's golden age

After Muhammad's death, the Islamic world was led by a succession of caliphs (caliph means "successor"). The caliphs waged many wars in order to defend and spread Islam. From 661, Islam was led by the Omayyad rulers in Damascus. A golden age of Islamic culture lasted from 750 to 1258.

During this period, Islam was led by the Abbasid rulers in Baghdad.

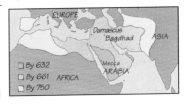

Regions where Islam had spread by 750

c.790
Viking raids

By 790, the people of western Europe were threatened by an enemy from the north – the Vikings. The Vikings were seafarers from Scandinavia. Some wanted to trade, but others wanted to loot and settle new lands.

The Vikings journeyed as far as Baghdad in the east and North America in the west. They eventually merged with local people and the raids stopped around 1100.

A Viking warrior and his battle flag

13

800
Charlemagne crowned

The greatest king in Europe in the eighth century was called Charles the Great, or Charlemagne. He was King of the Franks and he built the largest empire in Europe since the Romans. He fought the pagans (people who did not believe in the Christian God) and converted them to Christianity. The Pope crowned him "King of the Romans" in 800.

Charlemagne

860
Rurik the Rus

The Vikings from Scandinavia settled in many places, including Russia. The Russian Slavs and the Arabs called the Vikings the "Rus". This is how Russia got its name. It is said that in a desperate attempt to bring peace, the Slavs invited three Rus brothers to rule them around the year 860. Soon after this one of them, called Rurik, seized his brothers' lands and created a new kingdom based around the city of Novgorod. This was the first Russian state.

A Viking trader

1066
The Norman Conquest

In 1066, William of Normandy conquered the English at the Battle of Hastings. The Normans became the feudal overlords of the English and William became King of England.

In Europe, the period from around 1050 to 1450 is known as the Middle Ages. A society known as the feudal system was common during this time. Lords built castles and employed knights to defend the people. In return the people worked on the lords' land.

William the Conqueror

1088
Bologna – the first university

In the Middle Ages, there were many monks and nuns who devoted their lives to God. To train churchmen, monks ran the first schools which later developed into universities. The first university in Europe opened in Bologna, Italy in 1088.

14

Saladin, who led the Muslims against the Third Crusade (1189-92).

1096
The First Crusade

In the eleventh century, a group of Muslims called the Seljuk Turks conquered Palestine (the Holy Land), barring the way of Christians who wanted to visit the area.

This led to a period of fighting between Muslims and Christians, who marched from Europe in an effort to regain the Holy Land. They set off in huge numbers in campaigns known as the Crusades. The First Crusade set off in 1096. There were seven crusades in all, the last taking place in 1270.

1242
The Battle of Lake Peipus

In the thirteenth century, northern Russia was invaded by the Swedes and the Teutonic Knights (a military and religious order of German knights).

The Russian hero, Alexander of Novgorod, fought off these attacks. In 1242, he defeated the Teutonic Knights on the frozen Lake Peipus, where his mounted enemies were so heavy that they fell through the frozen ice. The lighter Russian soldiers survived.

1258
The Mongols sack Baghdad

In the thirteenth century, the Mongols from the east threatened the Islamic world. In 1258, they sacked Baghdad and murdered the last Abbasid caliph by rolling him up in a carpet and letting horses trample him to death. The Mongol advance was halted when the Egyptian Marmelukes defeated them at the Battle of Ain Jalut in 1261.

Mongol fighter

15

1259
The Hanseatic League

In the Middle Ages, towns grew and prospered all over Europe. Trade increased and a group of cities in northern Europe set up an association to protect their trade. The association was called the Hanseatic League and it flourished between 1259 and 1358.

A trading port in northern Europe

1279
The Mongols conquer China

The Mongols were a tough fighting force who, under Genghis Khan, conquered a massive empire from the edges of Europe to China in the east. In 1279, under Genghis's grandson Kublai Khan, they completed their conquest of China. Kublai Khan became Emperor of China. He set up a magnificent court in Khanbalik (modern Beijing).

Kublai Khan also tried to invade Japan, but failed twice. After his death, the Chinese drove the Mongols out.

Kublai Khan, Mongol emperor from 1260 to 1294

1339
Ashikaga Period in Japan

Japan was ruled by an emperor, but the government was run by a military leader called a *shogun*. In 1339 Japan entered the Ashikaga Period, which lasted until 1573. During this time, the *shoguns* lost control over the landowners, called *daimyos*. The *daimyos* continually fought each other, employing large armies of fierce warriors, known as *samurai*.

A samurai warrior

1339
The Hundred Years' War

Europe suffered many wars in the Middle Ages, but the longest was the Hundred Years' War. It was fought on and off between England and France from 1339 to 1453. Although the English won some great victories, including the Battle of Agincourt in 1415, they were eventually pushed out of France. Only Calais remained English.

An English archer

1347
The Black Death rages

In 1347, a terrible disease called the bubonic plague swept across Europe. Known as the Black Death, it killed a third of the entire population. So many died that there weren't enough workers to tend the fields. Food prices were high and great hardship was suffered by the poor.

Clothes belonging to plague victims were burned to stop the disease.

c.1350
Palace at Zimbabwe

Around 1350 a great palace, known as Great Zimbabwe, was built in the town of Zimbabwe in southern Africa. Zimbabwe was a wealthy place which sent iron, ivory and gold to the trading ports on the east coast of Africa. They were then shipped to the Middle East, India and China. The modern country of Zimbabwe is named after this ancient capital.

1368
The Ming Dynasty begins

In 1368, a family of rulers called the Ming Dynasty took control of China. Under the Ming, China enjoyed 150 years of prosperity and peace. The Ming were famous for their porcelain and also planted wonderful gardens and built magnificent tombs for their rulers. Eventually the state fell apart, due to many rebellions.

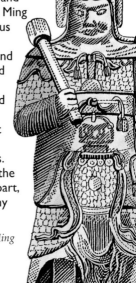
A marble Ming statue

17

c.1380
The Renaissance begins

In Europe in the late fourteenth to the sixteenth centuries, there was a great revival in arts, science and the learning of Ancient Greece and Rome.

This idea for a flying machine was designed by Renaissance painter, sculptor and scientist, Leonardo da Vinci (1452-1519).

This new spirit of learning and questioning began in Italy and spread rapidly throughout Europe. It is known as the Renaissance, meaning "rebirth".

1389
The Battle of Kossova

In 1389, the Ottoman Turks won the Battle of Kossova against the Byzantines, which gave them control of the Balkans in southeast Europe. The Ottomans continued to carve out a huge empire and they even captured the city of Constantinople in 1453, bringing to an end the last stronghold of the old Roman Empire.

1462
Reign of Ivan III begins

In the fourteenth century, Moscow became the dominant Russian state. Its size and importance

Ivan III

grew during the reign of Ivan III, the Great, who reigned from 1462 to 1505. He conquered the territory of Novgorod and refused to pay tribute (payment to prevent attack) to the Tartars, making Russia independent from them at last. Russian rulers took the title Czar (Caesar).

1492
Christopher Columbus

In 1492, Christopher Columbus set out to prove that he could reach India in the east by sailing west. But, instead he landed in America, which lay in his path. He called the place where he landed the Indies, believing that he had indeed reached India.

Columbus's voyage to America paved the way for the rise of the great empires of Spain and Portugal, soon to conquer vast areas of America.

1517
The Reformation begins

Martin Luther

By the sixteenth century, some people were criticizing the Roman Catholic Church, which they believed was in need of reform. One of the first people to do this, in 1517, was a monk named Martin Luther. Luther's followers became known as Protestants. Although Protestants ran the risk of persecution, they eventually began to set up their own churches across Europe. This period is called the Reformation.

1519
Magellan

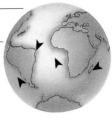

Magellan's route

In 1519, the first voyage around the world was led by Ferdinand Magellan. This era saw many voyages of discovery to Africa, Asia and America.

1519
Cortez conquers the Aztecs

The Aztecs controlled a large area of Central America and were continually at war with nearby peoples. They had a large, well-organized empire, beautiful cities, strict laws and complex religious beliefs. In 1519, they were conquered by Spanish invaders led by Hernan Cortez.

An Aztec god

1520
Suleiman the Magnificent

In 1520 Sultan Suleiman I, the Magnificent, came to the Ottoman throne. His reign saw the peak in Ottoman power and the empire had reached its greatest extent by his death in 1566. In 1571, however, the Ottomans were beaten at sea at the Battle of Lepanto by a league of Europeans. From then on, Ottoman power declined.

Suleiman the Magnificent

1532
The Incas

The Incas had a great empire. They controlled a large area of South America. In 1532, they were conquered by the Spaniards, led by Francisco Pizarro. Their territory, like that of the Aztecs, became a Spanish colony. Spain became rich from the plentiful supplies of gold and silver found in America.

A Spanish conqueror, or conquistador

1600
The Battle of Sekigahara

In 1600, a great battle took place in Japan, at Sekigahara. An important *daimyo* (landowner) called Tokugawa Ieyasu took the title *Shogun*. The title was a military one, but the holder ran the government too. Ieyasu limited the power of the other *daimyos* and his descendents kept the title of *Shogun* until 1868.

Tokugawa Ieyasu

1618
The Thirty Years' War

In 1618, a war broke out when Bohemia, part of the Holy Roman Empire (which had a Catholic Emperor), chose a Protestant king instead of a Catholic one. War broke out, with Catholic Spain and Austria on one side and German Protestants on the other. For thirty years, war raged across Germany and many people were driven away or killed.

1620
The Pilgrim Fathers set sail

The Pilgrims arriving in their new home – North America.

In 1620, a group of Protestants from England set sail for America on board a ship called the *Mayflower*. They did not agree with England's religious policy and wanted to live where they could worship in their own way. They landed at Plymouth Rock, Massachusetts and set up a colony. Roman Catholics also set up a colony in Maryland to escape persecution in England.

1643
Louis XIV of France reigns

France entered a golden age during the reign of Louis XIV, from 1643-1715. His court was splendidly wealthy and he was known as the Sun King. Louis saw himself as Europe's leader. He fought several campaigns to extend his territory.

Louis XIV performing in a ballet

c.1645
The Manchu Dynasty

In the mid-1640s, the Chinese invited Manchu warriors from the north into China to help them defend themselves against bandits. Soon, however, the Manchus established themselves as rulers in China. The Manchu Empire grew.

In the eighteenth century, western nations wanted to trade with China, but the Chinese wanted nothing to do with them. By the nineteenth century, though, European influence had weakened China.

The dragon – the ancient symbol of China

21

1654
The Taj Mahal is built

In the sixteenth century, a group of Muslims called the Moguls carved out a fabulous empire in India. The famous monument, the Taj Mahal, was built by the Mogul Emperor Shah Jahan in 1654. The empire survived until the eighteenth century, when conflicts within it caused it to collapse.

The Taj Mahal

1667
The naming of New York

In the seventeenth century, the Spaniards, English, French and Dutch all founded colonies in North America. After a war in 1667, the Dutch had to surrender their colonies to the English. The Dutch town of New Amsterdam was then renamed New York.

1689
Peter the Great reigns

Russia entered a golden age under the reign of Peter the Great, who reigned from 1689-1725. He was determined to modernize Russia.

Peter began a system of reforms. In order to learn as much as possible, he journeyed around Europe, training in navigation and in shipbuilding. He brought foreign craftsmen to Russia and founded a new capital – St. Petersburg.

c.1750
The Industrial Revolution

Around 1750, a great change began in Britain. Due to the invention of new machinery, goods were manufactured quicker and cheaper in factories, rather than in people's homes. Towns and cities grew as people left their villages to work in the new factories.

A Newcomen steam engine – one of the first steam-powered machines

Transportation improved and so did methods of power production. This great change is called the Industrial Revolution. It had spread across Europe and to America by the end of the nineteenth century.

1762
Catherine the Great reigns

In 1762, Catherine II, the Great, came to the Russian throne. She had married the heir to the Russian throne, but he was very unpopular and was murdered. Catherine took over and under her rule, the Russian Empire grew and St. Petersburg became a magnificent city.

1770
Cook lands in Australia

In 1768, Englishman James Cook began the first of three famous voyages of discovery to Australia, New Zealand and around the Pacific Ocean. Although Europeans had sailed near to Australia before, in 1770 he was the first actually to land there. He named his landing spot Botany Bay. On Cook's second voyage (1772-1775) he visited Easter Island in the Pacific Ocean – the farthest south yet reached by a European. On his third voyage, Cook was killed in a dispute with local people in Hawaii.

Giant stone heads on Easter Island

1759
The Battle of Quebec

The French and the British were great rivals in North America. In 1759 the British General James Wolfe captured the French town of Quebec in Canada. This paved the way for the complete conquest of Canada by the British in the following year.

23

1776
Birth of the United States

George Washington

By the early eighteenth century, Britain had 13 colonies on the east coast of America. In 1775, war broke out between Britain and the colonists, who wanted independence. In 1776 the Declaration of Independence was made and the 13 colonies became the United States. The colonists, led by George Washington, were eventually victorious and independence was recognized in 1783.

1789
The French Revolution

In 1789, a revolution against the king and the nobility broke out in France. Ordinary people were unhappy with their lot and were angry at the wealth of the upper classes.

Nobles were executed after the revolution.

The revolution became very bloody – the king, queen and many nobles were executed within a period of a few months, known as the Reign of Terror.

1804
Napoleon Bonaparte

In 1804, Napoleon Bonaparte became Emperor of France. He began his career as a lowly soldier, but gradually rose through the ranks. Once he became emperor, he conquered much of Europe in a series *Napoleon* of brilliant campaigns. Other European nations joined forces to defeat him and he was eventually forced to abdicate in 1814. In 1815, he briefly came to power once more, but was finally beaten at the Battle of Waterloo. He later died in exile.

1823
The slave trade is banned

In the sixteenth century a trade in African slaves had begun, growing in scale and profit. Ships sailed from Europe to Africa, where they picked up slaves. They shipped them to the Americas where they were exchanged for goods such as cotton. In 1823, William Wilberforce succeeded in passing a law banning slavery in the British Empire.

Independence for South America

Between around 1810 and 1830, the South American nations gained their independence. Spain and Portugal between them had owned all of South America since they colonized it in the sixteenth century. This was the first region of the world to shake off European colonizers.

The Gold Rush

At first, only trappers, hunters and explorers journeyed west of the Mississippi River in North America. Then in 1848, gold was discovered in California on the west coast. Miners set out over the wilderness to reach the gold mines. They faced great danger, including lack of food and attacks by the American Indians. The gold rush soon died, but people still went west to farm and settle.

North American Indians from the Great Plains in the west

Revolutions across Europe

In 1848 there were rebellions all over Europe as people rose up against their rulers. This was the result of a growing demand for greater democracy – the right to vote. There was also a growing feeling of nationalism – a feeling shared by people of one area that they are bound together by a common language, religion, culture and history. Everywhere in Europe, people wanted a greater say in the government of their country.

Garibaldi, the nationalist who led the Italians against their Austrian rulers.

The scramble for Africa

In the nineteenth century, a race began to bring the different areas of Africa under European influence. This race, was known as the "scramble for Africa". Algeria, colonized by France in 1830, was one of the first areas in Africa to become a colony. By the end of the century, nearly all of the continent was colonized, Britain and France having the most territory.

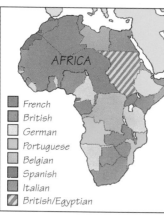

French
British
German
Portuguese
Belgian
Spanish
Italian
British/Egyptian

European colonies in Africa by the early twentieth century

1861

Freedom for the serfs

In Russia, serfs (peasants) were slaves under control of their local nobleman. In the nineteenth century, Russian noblemen argued about whether or not to free them.

Meanwhile, the serfs continued to suffer cruelty and hardship. At last in 1861, Alexander II issued a law freeing 20 million people. The newly-freed serfs, however, had to pay for their land.

A Russian serf

1861

The American Civil War

In 1861 war broke out between the northern and the southern states of the USA. One of the many issues that divided them was slavery, which the North disagreed with but which the South relied on for its workforce. The South tried to leave the Union and form the Confederate States of America, but the North fought them to prevent this.

In 1863 President Abraham Lincoln declared all slaves to be free. This was followed in 1865 by victory for the North.

1876
Battle of Little Big Horn

As settlers claimed more and more land in North America, battles were fought between the US army and the North American Indians. Although the Indians were eventually beaten, they did win some victories, including the Battle of Little Big Horn in 1876. General Custer

General Custer

and over two hundred men attacked a well-prepared ambush and were slaughtered.

1877
Victoria becomes Empress of India

In 1877, the British Queen Victoria was declared Empress of India. Britain was a powerful nation and its colonies spanned the globe.

British officers in India

Britain owned territory from the Caribbean in the west to the vastly rich India in the east.

1893
First votes for women

Arrest of a woman campaigner

The first country to give the vote to women was New Zealand in 1893. Other countries, however, were slow to follow. During World War One, many women took on jobs traditionally filled by men. This proved to men that women were responsible members of society. Votes for women followed in 1919 in Britain and 1920 in the USA.

1899
The Boxer Rebellion

In Beijing, China in 1899, a rebellion broke out against foreigners that lasted for several months. This was caused by resentment at the way China was being influenced by foreign powers. The rebellion was organized by a secret society called the Boxers, supported by the Dowager Empress, Tz'u H'si. An international force was sent to defeat the Boxers and from then on, foreigners could enter China more freely.

A Boxer rebel

1901
Australia becomes a nation

On January 1, 1901, the six British colonies in Australia were united to form the Commonwealth of Australia. This had been debated for 50 years, but was finally agreed due to worries about colonization and immigration by other nations. It wasn't until 1909 that a site for a capital at Canberra was agreed.

1914
World War One breaks out

In 1914 World War One broke out in Europe. Tensions had been rising for some time and now the major powers lined up against each other – Britain, France and Russia against Germany and Austria-Hungary. The war lasted for four years and ended in victory for Britain and France. The war included some of the bloodiest battles ever known, such as the Battle of the Somme in 1916 which lasted for five months and killed over 1.2 million men.

1917
The Russian Revolution

Lenin, the first Soviet leader

The Russian people were poor and disillusioned with their rulers, so in 1917 they rebelled. The Czar abdicated and was later executed with his family. After this, different groups struggled to control the Russian Empire.

By 1922 the civil war ended and a group called the Bolsheviks took power. They set up a communist government (based on state control and in which people were held to be equal) and renamed their empire the Soviet Union.

German World War One fighter plane

28

1929
The Wall Street Crash

In 1929, the value of stocks and shares on the New York Stock Exchange in Wall Street dropped dramatically. Many people lost large amounts of money overnight. Businesses were ruined and this caused a worldwide depression, in which millions lost their jobs and suffered great hardship.

The New York Stock Exchange

The German leader, Adolf Hitler, planned to dominate Europe and in 1939, war broke out with Britain and France. Fighting spread to Asia and Africa and involved more nations than any war before. Although Germany very nearly won the war, it was finally defeated in 1945.

1945
The Holocaust is discovered

When the war ended, it was discovered that Hitler had set up concentration camps, where millions of Jews and other people despised by the German Nazi Party had been murdered. At least twelve million people, six million of them Jews, were killed in this way. This event is known as the Holocaust.

1939
World War Two

During the 1930s, Italy, Spain and Germany were ruled by fascist governments, which believed in state control of people's lives and also strong nationalism.

German army motorcycle rider from World War Two

1945
The atomic bomb is dropped

Japan, Germany's ally, continued to fight. The USA, Britain's ally, inflicted a swift defeat on Japan by dropping two atomic bombs on Hiroshima and Nagasaki in August 1945. Both cities were the scenes of terrible death and destruction.

Atomic bomb explosion

The start of the Cold War

After World War Two, the most powerful nations in the world were the Soviet Union and the USA, known as the superpowers. They became very suspicious of one another and their relationship became so bad that they opposed each other in politics and economics, and supported each other's enemies. This situation was known as the Cold War. It finally came to an end in the early 1990s, as communism in the Soviet Union began to break down slowly.

1947
Independence for India

After World War Two, Europe was nearly bankrupt and could no longer maintain its colonial empires. The colonies wanted self-government and a period began when many of them gained independence. India was the first to do so, in 1947. An organization called the Indian National Congress Party had been campaigning for independence for many years. The separate Muslim state of Pakistan was also created at the same time.

Gandhi, leader of the Indian National Congress Party

1948
Birth of Israel

In 1948, there was a crisis in Palestine. Arab Palestinians resented the presence of Jews, who had been arriving steadily in great numbers. Both groups regarded Palestine as their home. The United Nations organization created a new Jewish state of Israel in Palestine. Decades of violence followed.

1969
Man lands on the Moon

In 1969, American Neil Armstrong became the first man to set foot on the Moon. Along with fellow astronauts Edwin Aldrin and Michael Collins, Armstrong had been launched into space aboard the spacecraft *Apollo 11*. In all, he and Aldrin spent around two and a half hours on the Moon's surface.

Aldrin on the Moon

1989
Tiananmen Square massacre

In response to greater democracy in other countries around the world, calls for elections in communist China gathered strength in the late 1980s.

30

In 1989, 100,000 students demonstrated in Tiananmen Square in Beijing, the capital. The government stopped the demonstration with force and thousands were killed in Beijing and across China.

The Soviet Union ends

On December 31, 1991, the Soviet Union came to an end. Turmoil from economic reforms and calls for independence from its member republics had weakened the state. As the new republics gained independence, fighting between rival groups broke out in many of them.

The old Soviet flag (left) and the flag of Russia

The Rio Summit

In 1992, representatives from governments and organizations in many different countries came together at a huge conference in Rio de Janeiro, Brazil, to discuss the world's environmental problems.

The blue whale – an endangered species

The Rio Summit received a lot of publicity and caused people to realize that they should prevent harm to the Earth, its plants and animals, so that the environment is safe for the future.

The end of apartheid

In 1948, a system had been set up in South Africa which separated the different races.

An anti-apartheid poster

Called apartheid, it ensured that whites received advantages, while nonwhites had few rights. Other countries tried to force South Africa to abandon apartheid, but it refused. The system was finally dismantled in 1994 by President F.W. de Klerk. Soon after, Nelson Mandela became the country's first black president.

Index

Acknowledgements

This book is illustrated by: Philip Argent, Peter Dennis, Richard Draper, Nicholas Hewetson, Ian Jackson, John Lawrence, Ross Watton and Gerald Wood.

This book includes material previously published in *The Ancient World, Kings and Queens, World History Dates, the Atlas of World History* and *Europe.* First published in 1996 by Usborne Publishing Ltd, Usborne House, 83-85 Saffron Hill, London, EC1N 8RT. Copyright © Usborne Publishing Ltd 1996, 1995, 1993, 1991, 1987

First published in America March 1997 UE